GHOST DETECTORS

Tell No One!

BOOK 3

BY
DOTTI ENDERLE

ILLUSTRATED BY
HOWARD MCWILLIAM

magic
wagon

visit us at www.abdopublishing.com

A special thanks to Melissa Markham — DE
For my parents — HM

Published by Magic Wagon, a division of the ABDO Group,
8000 West 78th Street, Edina, Minnesota 55439. Copyright
© 2010 by Abdo Consulting Group, Inc. International copyrights
reserved in all countries. All rights reserved. No part of this
book may be reproduced in any form without written permission
from the publisher.

Calico Chapter Books™ is a trademark and logo of Magic Wagon.

Printed in the United States.

Text by Dotti Enderle
Illustrations by Howard McWilliam
Edited by Stephanie Hedlund and Rochelle Baltzer
Cover and interior design by Jaime Martens

Library of Congress Cataloging-in-Publication Data

Enderle, Dotti, 1954-
  Tell no one! / by Dotti Enderle ; illustrated by Howard
McWilliam.
      p. cm. -- (Ghost Detectors ; bk. 3)
  Summary: Ten-year-olds Malcolm and Dandy think their ghost-
hunting days are over when they start fifth grade with the
toughest teacher in their school, but Malcolm's photographs for
the yearbook reveal that the school is haunted.
  ISBN 978-1-60270-692-7
  [1. Ghosts--Fiction. 2. Haunted places--Fiction. 3. Schools--
Fiction. 4. Teachers--Fiction. 5. Photography--Fiction. 6. Family
life--Fiction. 7. Humorous stories.] I. McWilliam, Howard,
1977- ill. II. Title.
  PZ7.E69645Tel 2009
  [Fic]--dc22
                              2008055333

Contents

The Day Before

Malcolm and his best friend, Dandy, sat quietly in Malcolm's basement lab. It was one of those late afternoons, right before dinner, when you wish there were more hours left to hang out. Malcolm was perched on an old desk, while Dandy slumped lazily in a beanbag chair.

"I can't believe it went by so fast," Malcolm complained. He flipped on his Ecto-Handheld-Automatic-Heat-Sensitive-

Laser-Enhanced Specter Detector. It was the gadget he used for hunting ghosts.

With the specter detector on, he could play with his new dog, Spooky. Spooky was a phantom canine that had recently followed Malcolm home. He eagerly wagged his tail at Malcolm.

"I can't believe summer is already over," Malcolm said, as he put his chin in his hand. "It seems like we just started ghost hunting yesterday."

"Summer always goes fast," Dandy reminded him.

"Yeah, but this one went too fast." His hangdog expression practically touched the floor.

"Look at the bright side," Dandy said. "We're fifth graders this year."

That was true. Malcolm did like the

idea of being in the highest grade at Waxberry Elementary.

Dandy chewed a fingernail. "I bet fifth grade will be a lot harder than fourth."

"Yeah," Malcolm agreed.

"But we'll get to ride in the very back of the bus," Dandy continued.

"That's the bumpiest part!" Malcolm said.

Dandy suddenly sat forward. "Oh no, I just remembered—fifth graders have the last lunch of the day!"

Malcolm shook his head. "Let's hope there's enough food left."

Dandy looked like he'd just dropped his last piece of gum on the floor. The only lively creature in the basement was Malcolm's ghostly pet. *Yip! Yip!* Spooky hopped and bounced, jumping at Malcolm to play.

Malcolm scooted off the desk, onto the floor. Spooky tried to grab Malcolm's shirt for tug-of-war, but his teeth went right through the shirt.

Once Spooky learned he couldn't hang on, he decided a game of run-through-Malcolm would be more fun. He dashed in and out, one side then the other.

"Stop, Spooky. That tickles! Sit!"

Spooky sat eagerly, tail wagging.

Malcolm looked at Dandy and sighed. "You know the worst part of going back to school?"

Dandy slid another finger in his mouth and chewed on that nail. "There's something worse than 12:45 lunch?"

"We can only ghost hunt on weekends."

Malcolm and Dandy had already had two exciting ghost adventures this summer. First, they'd gone into the Freaky McBleaky house and been chased out by the ghost Herbert McBleaky. Malcolm still cringed at the thought of the major wedgie the jokester had given him.

Then, Malcolm waited weeks for his Ecto-Handheld-Automatic-Heat-Sensitive-Laser-Enhanced Ghost Zapper to arrive.

When it finally did, he went ghost hunting again. He zapped a ghost at the Millers' house—and met his late great-grandfather and Spooky!

"And we were just getting started," Dandy said.

Malcolm fidgeted with his specter detector, flipping it off and on. Spooky flicked off and on, too. He faded then returned, over and over, as the specter detector detected him.

"We won't let it end. Ghost hunting is what we do," Malcolm said, trying to sound encouraging. "We'll devote every weekend to searching out ghosts."

"Right," Dandy agreed.

"Nothing will stand in our way."

Dandy straightened, chin high. "Yep. Nothing."

Malcolm was starting to cheer up. "On weekends, ghost hunting comes first!"

"Right," Dandy said. "Ghost hunting comes first. Right after I do my homework . . . mow the lawn . . . clean my room . . . and bathe the dog." He counted out each item on his fingers.

Malcolm's cheerful mood quickly drooped. "We'll find time."

It was then that the basement door burst open. A voice much like a bullhorn blared, "Mom says it's time for dinner, snothead!"

Malcolm's sister, Cocoa, stood at the top of the stairs. She wore Irish green eye shadow and clown red lip gloss. Malcolm thought she looked like a traffic light.

Spooky was scared by Cocoa's demanding presence. He dashed straight through Malcolm and hid behind him.

"Tell Mom I'll be there in a minute," Malcolm said.

Cocoa glared, hands on hips. "I'm not your messenger. Now come eat. And tell your goofy friend he has to go home." Her lips curled into a devilish grin. "It's a school night."

He couldn't think of anything clever to say, so Malcolm simply stuck out his tongue.

"Nerd!" Cocoa yelled, stomping away.

Malcolm turned to Dandy. "There is one good thing about going back to school tomorrow."

"What's that?" Dandy wondered.

"Seven full hours away from her!"

Up and At 'Em

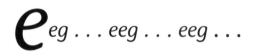

*e*eg . . . *eeg* . . . *eeg* . . .

The only sound worse than Cocoa's annoying screech was that of the alarm clock. The sound made Malcolm want to shed his skin. He slapped the off button and tumbled out of bed.

His plan to visit the bathroom failed when he discovered his sister had made camp in there.

"You're not the only person in this house, you know!" Malcolm loudly reminded her.

"It's the first day of school!" she called back through the closed door. "I have to look perfect!"

"If that's what you're waiting for, you'll be in there for eternity," Malcolm muttered as he walked away.

He tried his parents' bathroom, but Grandma Eunice occupied it. She'd obviously finished her morning prunes.

Malcolm gave up and headed to the kitchen for breakfast. He dropped two pieces of bread into the toaster. While he waited, he remembered the time he'd tried converting that very toaster into an alien heat ray.

When the toast was ready, he poured a glass of orange juice. His mom had

already put the peanut butter and bananas on the table.

Malcolm plopped into his chair. It scraped as he scooted closer. His parents were still eating, and they glanced up at all the noise he was making.

"I can't believe my babies are growing up so fast," Malcolm's mom said. Her voice was as sweet as the apple-mint jelly she smeared on her muffin.

His dad just grunted. Malcolm guessed he hadn't had a chance at the bathroom either.

"And it's already the first day of school," Mom continued.

"Please, don't remind me," Malcolm said, sipping some juice.

Mom sniffed the air. "It even smells like the first day. I can smell the newly

sharpened pencils, chalk dust, and Big Chief tablets."

"What are Big Chief tablets?"

"That's what we used when your dad and I were little. Right, dear?" she said to Dad.

Dad grunted again. He never looked up from staring at his coffee.

The bathroom door flew open, rattling the entire house. "MOM!" Cocoa shrieked.

She stood in the doorway, wearing a violet shirt, purple skirt, plum-colored hoop earrings, and lavender tie-dyed sneakers. The indigo tint of her nail polish, eye shadow, and lip gloss looked like something from the "undead" cosmetic line.

Cocoa reminded Malcolm of an enormous grape. If she stood there for

about 40 years, she could pass for a California raisin.

"Mom!" she whined this time. "Look!" She held out her shirt and pointed near the hem.

"What is it, sweetie?" Mom asked.

"Look!" Cocoa said again.

Mom squinted. "Look at what?"

Cocoa moved closer. "This!"

Mom squinted more. "I don't see anything."

"Of course not! The rhinestone heart fell off!" Cocoa drooped and sobbed like she just flunked history or something. Tears gushed down her cheeks. Malcolm didn't see what the big deal was, but that was a girl for you.

"No one will notice," Mom assured her soothingly.

"That's what I'm afraid of!" Cocoa stomped her foot. "No one will notice this awesome outfit."

Malcolm didn't know about awesome. But now that Cocoa was no longer blocking the doorway, he saw his chance at the bathroom. Before he could move a muscle, Cocoa whipped around.

"Now I have to rethink the whole thing. I must look perfect for the first day!" she yelled. She clomped back to the bathroom, slamming the door.

"Hey!" Malcolm called. "Your clothes are in your bedroom!"

"But crying smeared my makeup, dufus. I have to redo it!"

For once Malcolm looked forward to his first day of school—just so he could use the boys' room!

Slow Ride

The back of the school bus was indeed the bumpiest part. Malcolm wondered if the bus driver, Mr. Mullins, actually aimed for every pothole in the road. The boys were trapped in the far corner amid a crowd of chattering students.

Dandy yawned. "It's bumpy and hot back here. It's not as great as I thought it would be."

"No kidding," Malcolm said. He tried

pulling down a window, but no amount of tugging would free it.

Malcolm gave up and slumped down in his seat. But then he remembered something important. He reached into his backpack and pulled out his digital camera.

"What's that for?" Dandy asked. Sweat beads had formed on his nose like teeny raindrops.

"Pictures," Malcolm answered. "This year we're part of the yearbook staff, remember?"

Malcolm hadn't really wanted to be on the yearbook staff, but he was talked into it because they needed a photographer.

At first he'd resisted, but then he imagined all the cool things he could do with the photos. There was no limit to the fancy photo effects he could dream up.

He was already planning to swap the principal's head with the school mascot, a hornet. And he may even add bubbles to the noses of the student council. Malcolm was set to make this year's Waxberry Elementary yearbook the best ever.

Dandy scratched his nose, smearing the dirty sweat. "I don't know how to put together a yearbook."

"It's not hard. Remember when we were in kindergarten, and we made those placemats for Thanksgiving?" Malcolm asked.

Dandy nodded, looking confused. His finger slipped around to the other side of his nose. "Yeah. We glued old photos to a piece of construction paper."

"Well, it's sort of the same thing," Malcolm explained, playing with the strap of the camera.

Dandy's finger slid from his nose to his lip. He kept scratching. "But I ended up with more paste on the top than on the bottom. Everyone on my placemat had a milk mustache."

Milk mustaches . . . *Got Homework?* That was a great idea for the faculty picture!

"I don't think I'm going to be very good at working on the yearbook," Dandy added.

"Don't worry, Dandy. You can be my assistant and help me take pictures."

"That's no good. I usually end up with pictures of my fingers," Dandy said.

That was true. Malcolm remembered several years ago when he had found a footprint so large it could only have belonged to Bigfoot. It was starting to rain, so right then was his only chance to show proof. He'd lain down next to the huge track to give it scale. Then he had Dandy snap the photo.

When they uploaded the photos, Dandy's big orangey thumb covered the entire footprint. Malcolm had looked like he was being slammed by a giant meteor.

"How about I do the picture taking," Malcolm suggested. "You can pose the subjects."

Dandy sat forward, resting his elbows on his knees. "I guess I could do that."

"Of course you can. You'll be great at it," Malcolm encouraged his friend.

The bus bounced and jolted its way around a few more blocks, stopping every couple of minutes to cram in more kids. Then the Waxberry marquee came into view.

Welcome back to Waxberry for another great year! Go Hornets!

Some of the kids cheered. Some groaned. Dandy yawned. The first thing Malcolm did after he got off the bus was snap a picture of the marquee. He had big plans for the yearbook photos. Nothing was going to mess that up.

CLASSROOM
503

Grueling Goolsby

Malcolm snapped a few more pictures of the morning bustle. He caught kids rushing to class and teachers smiling through clenched teeth on film.

He also caught Coss Fitzfox, last year's Kickball King, hobbling in on crutches. He snapped a picture of "Booger" McCready, chess champion, walking the halls with a pair of soccer cleats slung over his shoulder. And he captured

Waxberry's rough-and-ready tomboy, Candace Dillion, wearing mascara.

"You can't make this stuff up," Malcolm told Dandy. They headed for the bulletin board in the cafeteria to check which rooms they were assigned.

"I hope we're in the same class again," Dandy said, heaving his enormous backpack. With every step he appeared to be trudging through syrup.

It didn't take long to find their names. "Look!" Dandy said. "We are in the same room."

Malcolm smiled. "Yep." Then he checked the room number. Yikes! Room 503! Mrs. Goolsby! Grueling Goolsby, the toughest teacher in the entire school.

"Oh no! We're doomed." Dandy dropped his backpack with a thud.

Malcolm couldn't agree more.

Dandy dragged his backpack behind him as they headed for that fateful room.

Mrs. Goolsby stood by the classroom door. She tapped a ruler on her palm as students ducked in. Malcolm figured she couldn't wait to shut the door and begin the torture.

Malcolm debated whether or not to take her picture. *Not a good idea*, he concluded.

When they took their seats, Dandy whispered, "I guess we won't get to ghost hunt now, huh?"

True. There probably wouldn't be another free weekend until next summer. Malcolm had heard that Mrs. Goolsby even assigned homework during the winter holidays! "Maybe it won't be so bad," he said. But secretly, he knew better.

The sweat beads had returned to Dandy's nose. His eyes were filled with panic. "Maybe we could transfer out."

Malcolm shrugged. "Doubtful."

"Maybe our parents would agree to homeschool us."

"Even more doubtful," Malcolm said as the bell rang.

"Quiet!" Mrs. Goolsby called, the door sweeping shut. "Pull out your math books and turn to Chapter One."

Among the groans Dandy said, "But we haven't even heard the announcements."

"Who said that?" Mrs. Goolsby asked, her eyes piercing each person.

Dandy slowly raised a shaky hand.

"What is your name?" she demanded.

Dandy gulped. "Daniel. Daniel Dee."

"Well, Mr. Dee," Mrs. Goolsby sneered. "I bet you can do at least one problem before the announcements. Let's see, shall we?"

Dandy gulped again, much louder. "What about attendance?"

Mrs. Goolsby slapped the ruler hard across the edge of her desk, causing an

explosive noise that could've set off a panic bell. "It's my job to worry about attendance, Mr. Dee. It's your job to get those problems done. Stop wasting time!"

The kids scurried for their books and pencils. Malcolm saw Dandy staring at the blunt nub of his, and knew he was too frightened to get up and use the pencil sharpener.

They worked the math problems, only stopping to say the Pledge of Allegiance. Mrs. Goolsby strolled by each desk. She paused at Malcolm's desk. "What's this?" She held up the camera.

"I'm taking pictures for the yearbook," he answered.

"Are you taking pictures at this very moment?" she grilled.

"No," Malcolm said. Now he was doing the gulping.

"Then . . . put . . . it . . . away," she rolled out each word like she was speaking a foreign language.

Malcolm did as he was told.

As the day progressed, it didn't get much better. There were no introductory games in Mrs. Goolsby's class. No working in teams like in fourth grade. Just hour after hour of Math, English, Science, and History.

Malcolm did manage to take more pictures. But that was during lunch, recess, and Mrs. Flutterfly's art class. When the three o'clock bell rang, Malcolm was the first in line for the school bus. He couldn't wait to get home.

After a couple of cookies and lemonade, he relayed the dreadful events of the day to his mom. "Mrs. Goolsby's a velociraptor in loafers!" he said.

"Oh, Malcolm," Mom sighed. "You have such an imagination."

Malcolm knew he wasn't going to get any sympathy. So, he headed to the computer to upload the yearbook photos before he started his pile of homework.

He checked them one by one. Then, he checked them again. He looked at his camera, then back to the pictures on his computer. He zoomed in closer and checked again. Then Malcolm dashed to the phone.

"Dandy, get over here quick! Our ghost hunting days are not over!"

Tell No One!

"I don't get it," Dandy said, looking from the computer screen to the photo printouts. He twitched his nose like he was about to sneeze.

"I don't either," Malcolm said. "It's the weirdest thing that's ever happened to me."

Dandy gave him a look.

"Okay, maybe not the weirdest, but it comes pretty close."

"Who is that guy?" Dandy asked.

Malcolm had no idea. He looked at the photos again. The picture of the school marquee came out just fine. But instead of *Go Hornets!* it said *TELL NO ONE!* And next to the marquee stood an odd-looking man. Odd, for a couple reasons.

1. He wore a green khaki fishing cap and vest, both covered in various fishing hooks and lures.

2. The man was transparent. No doubt, a ghost!

Malcolm checked out the close-up he'd taken of Candace Dillion. He caught her mid-blink. But instead of eye makeup, there was writing on both her eyelids.

Left eyelid: *TELL*

Right eyelid: *NO ONE!*

And standing directly behind her was the ghostly fisherman.

Malcolm studied the photo of Booger McCready. Booger's T-shirt now sported the words, *TELL NO ONE!* The fisherman lurked nearby.

And the picture of Coss Fitzfox clearly showed *TELL NO ONE!* written across the cast on his leg. The phantom fisherman peeked over his shoulder.

Malcolm scrolled through the same photos on the computer. "The school is definitely haunted," he told Dandy.

"It could be a glitch in the camera," Dandy suggested.

"You mean like a mechanical failure?"

Daddy nodded. "Yeah. A glitch."

"I double-checked it, Dandy. Besides, a glitch would probably cause lots of blobs or something. Not this."

"Maybe it's a double-exposure."

"Of what?" Malcolm argued. "I've never taken any pictures with those words on them . . . or that guy. I've never seen him before. And digital cameras don't make double-exposures."

"Did you have your specter detector with you?" Dandy wondered.

Malcolm shook his head no. He picked up the detector and flipped it to On. He liked the sound it made warming up. Then he switched it to Detect.

Yip! Yip! Spooky appeared, as if he'd been patiently waiting to be noticed by the specter detector and Malcolm.

"Hey, Spooky! I missed you today."

The dog bounced and wagged his tail.

Dandy leaned down and pretended to pet the dog. His hand brushed completely

through the pooch, but Spooky's face showed he appreciated the gesture.

Malcolm went back to studying the photo. "I just wish I knew what this meant," he said.

Dandy continued fake-petting Spooky. "We'll have to figure it out later. Can you believe all the homework Mrs. Goolsby gave us? I'm going to be up way past my bedtime."

Malcolm groaned. "No kidding. And on the first day! What teacher assigns a 1,000-word essay on the lessons we learned over summer vacation and how they relate to the writings of Roald Dahl?"

"Mrs. Goolsby!" Dandy complained. Even Spooky let out a *Yip! Yip!*

Malcolm turned off his specter detector, sending Spooky back to invisible realms.

Then he and Dandy trudged up the steps of the basement lab.

"Even though we can't do it tonight, we have to find out who that guy is," Malcolm said. "We need to know why he's haunting the school."

"Well, whoever he is," Dandy said, "his instructions are clear. We can't tell anyone! And I'm not going to go against any ghost's wishes. . . ."

A Muddy Excuse

Malcolm took his camera to school early the next day. He took pictures of the marquee, the cafeteria, and the library before heading to class.

"I've got to test it," he told Dandy. "I've got to find out why he's haunting the school. I'm going to take as many pictures as I can."

Dandy's backpack looked even heavier than yesterday. His stroll down the hall looked more like a trek up a steep

mountain. "Maybe he used to be a school teacher or P.E. coach here."

"But why the fishing getup?" Malcolm reasoned. "Shouldn't he be haunting a lake house, or a fishing boat, or Angler Bob's Bait Shop instead?"

Dandy adjusted his backpack. As he did, his knees buckled a little. "Maybe there used to be a lake here, and the school was built over it."

"Don't be silly, Dandy. Where would they've put all the water?"

"Well, our toilets have been overflowing a lot."

As they were about to step into the classroom, Mrs. Goolsby cried, "Oh, no you don't!"

Malcolm and Dandy froze.

"Look at your shoes!" she yelled at them. Her face had flushed a heated pink, and her eyes zapped them like lasers. "Caked in mud! I will not have you soiling my classroom!"

The boys just looked at each other. Neither one was sure what to do. After all, they'd never seen a teacher so upset about a little dirt.

"Remove your shoes this instant," she instructed, "and set them by the door. You will spend your recess in the boys' room cleaning them. Understood?"

They both nodded, afraid to speak.

"Now take your seats!"

They scrambled to get their sneakers off. Once they were seated, Mrs. Goolsby drilled them through a morning of nonstop lectures, lessons, and practice

sheets. Malcolm wondered if it was possible for a person's brain to overload and short-circuit.

"Getting mud on our shoes turned out to be lucky," Malcolm told Dandy as the other kids lined up for recess.

Dandy scrunched his eyebrows. "Why was that lucky? She's scarier than the ghost fisherman!"

Malcolm grinned. "It was lucky because the computer lab is empty this time of day."

"We can't clean our shoes in the computer lab!" Dandy argued. "We'll get detention."

"We're not going to clean our shoes, silly," Malcolm said impatiently.

Panic flashed across Dandy's face. "If we don't clean our shoes, we'll get detention for sure!"

"We'll clean our shoes later. Follow me, we've got ghost hunting to do."

Dandy followed, trudging like he still had his backpack on. He held his dirty sneakers by the laces, letting them sway with each step. Dried dirt flew with every swing.

Malcolm carefully closed the door to the computer lab, then dug his camera out of his pants pocket.

"Oh, I get it," Dandy said.

Malcolm typed his school password into one of the computers, then connected the camera. It was no surprise when he checked the uploaded pictures.

In the first photo, the fisherman sat on top of the marquee. Today it had said: *Volleyball tryouts tonight! Go Hornets!* But *Tell No One!* had replaced *Go Hornets!* once again.

In the next photo, the fisherman was giving a droopy-eyed janitor bunny ears. The fisherman was grinning goofily, but the janitor had no idea. *Tell No One!* was now on the janitor's mop bucket.

In the library photo, he stood next to the 700 section. It seemed pretty fitting that he was in section where the "fishing for kids" books were shelved. He was holding up the book *Tell No One for Dummies*.

Malcolm wasn't surprised that every picture had the words *TELL NO ONE!* He just wished he knew what that meant.

"Malcolm, recess is almost over," Dandy whispered. "I'm way more scared of Mrs. Goolsby than of a ghost giving bunny ears. Can we go clean our shoes before the bell rings?"

Malcolm sighed. "Yeah, just give me another second." He printed out all three of the pictures and tucked them under his shirt. Then he and Dandy headed for the restroom to clean off their sneakers.

Fishing for Answers

Malcolm dropped his load of school books on the kitchen table, then looked over his homework assignments. *Maybe I should transfer to military school,* he thought. *It'd be a lot easier.* He plopped himself down in a chair.

The house was particularly quiet. Dad was still at work. Mom and Cocoa were out shopping for more new school clothes—even though they'd bought Cocoa a closetful last weekend! Girls!

Grandma Eunice came walking in, pushing her wheelchair in front of her. Everyone else in the family thought she was weak and had lost her mind. Grandma played along so she could get out of doing household chores, but Malcolm knew the truth. It was their secret.

"Grandma, why do you even own that stupid wheelchair? I know you don't need it."

Grandma turned the chair toward the table. "Your mom thinks I'm too weak to walk on my own. But, I keep it so I'll always have a chair handy." She demonstrated by sitting down. Then she took a banana from the bowl and began peeling.

"Look at all this homework," Malcolm said. "My new teacher is tough."

Grandma Eunice clacked her false teeth around, getting ready for a bite. "That's nothing," she stated. "Back in my day . . ."

Here we go again! Malcolm thought.

" . . . I had wake up at four AM to milk the cows before walking seven miles to school barefoot. The teacher would beat us with a rattlesnake if we were just five minutes tardy!"

"A rattlesnake?" Malcolm said, not believing it one bit.

"And we didn't have all those fancy computers and calculators. It was all done up here." She tapped the side of her head. A piece of yucky banana string stuck to her hair.

She went on, "You all whine and worry when your computers won't boot up. We whined and worried when our pencils

wore down. And we didn't have those gliding gel pens like your sister writes her love poems with."

Malcolm knew then that Grandma Eunice had been sneaking through Cocoa's things. It was about time, too. After all, she'd been borrowing his specter detector to find Grandpa Bertram all summer.

"We had fountain pens," she rumbled. "Fountain pens with inkwells. It was a mess! Splotchy papers . . . stained fingers and ink spots on your favorite clothes—"

"Yeah," Malcolm interrupted. "Those were the good old days."

"You're darn tooting!" Grandma said. She crammed the banana into her mouth and mushed down with her choppers.

Malcolm opened his science book. Science was his favorite subject—

especially the current lesson on mapping the constellations.

He tried to concentrate, but his mind kept straying back to the mysterious fisherman. Plus, Grandma Eunice was making outrageously loud smacking noises with her teeth.

 Malcolm looked up as she flung the banana peel over her shoulder, scoring a two-pointer as it hit the trash. He shook his head as she celebrated.

"Grandma," he started, "you're good at keeping secrets, right?"

Grandma Eunice shrugged. "Even if I told, who'd believe me?"

A good point, but still Malcolm hesitated. He wanted to show her the photos. He could use another opinion, but the messages clearly said *TELL NO ONE!* And if there was one thing Malcolm had learned in his lifetime, it was never take an exclamation point lightly. But then again . . .

"Does this have to do with your ghost hunting?" Grandma asked.

"Yeah," Malcolm said, sheepishly. He showed her the photos and updated her on what had happened so far. "Do you know him?"

Grandma shook her head. "No, I've never seen him before."

"Why do you think he keeps appearing if he doesn't want me to tell anyone?"

"You can't trust a fisherman, Malcolm. They'll make up a whopper of a fish tale without blinking. I remember once when Grandpa Bertram went fishing with some of his pals. Tried to convince me that he'd reeled up a barracuda, hopped on its back, and rode it like he was in the rodeo."

"And you didn't believe him?"

Grandma rolled her eyes. "That barracuda would be stuffed and hanging on the wall if it were true."

"So you think the ghost is making this up and really wants me to tell?" he asked, reaching up and plucking the banana string from her hair.

Grandma Eunice stared him straight in the eyes. "Maybe you should go ask him."

After thinking it over for about thirty seconds, Malcolm went to the phone and called Dandy. "We've got to go back to the school."

Dandy gasped. "Are you kidding me? Our weekly vocabulary list is longer than the dictionary, and I'm still trying to figure out how to connect the dots on these constellations."

"We can do our homework together later. Get your bike and meet me on the corner." Malcolm hung up and began gathering his supplies. He had fishing to do.

In and Out

Malcolm tugged on the school's front door. Locked. There were lights on, and a few people milled about inside. Finally, a teacher came over and pushed open the door.

"What do you need?" she asked.

"I forgot my homework," Malcolm fibbed. He couldn't tell her the truth. How do you explain to a teacher that you really need to make contact with a ghostly

fisherman to find out what it is he doesn't want you to tell? Much too complicated.

"In and out," the teacher said, holding the door open.

Malcolm and Dandy rushed by her, hurrying through the lobby and down the hall. They ducked into an empty classroom.

"What now?" Dandy wondered. "There are still teachers around."

Malcolm, busy digging his specter detector out of his backpack, said, "We'll just have to avoid them."

He flipped the switch to the On position. Someone passed by the doorway. The boys flattened themselves against the wall.

"Maybe we should've come at night," Dandy suggested. "When all the teachers were gone."

"That's when the janitors are here. No way they would let us in." Malcolm watched the warm-up light on his gadget, then flipped it to Detect.

Bleep, bleep, bleep, bleep, bleep!

It immediately picked up ghost activity.

The boys looked at each other and glanced around the empty classroom. Then . . .

Yip! Yip!

They both jumped with fright.

"Spooky!" Malcolm said softly. "You followed us?"

Yip! Yip! The dog happily bounced around like he was on springs.

"Go home," Malcolm ordered. "Now!"

Spooky, not the most obedient of ghost pets, raced in and out of Malcolm's feet. Literally!

"What are we going to do now?" Dandy asked.

"Good question," Malcolm said. "As long as Spooky's here the specter detector will bleep. We won't know if the fisherman is around until he actually appears."

"Yeah, and I don't want him sneaking up on me with a big old shark hook or something," Dandy added.

Spooky continued his hyper play.

"Settle down, boy," Malcolm warned. "We can't let anyone see you."

The boys stood, watching Spooky run in circles and yip at most everything.

"We've got to do something," Malcolm finally said. "The longer we stay here, the better our chances of getting caught."

Dandy rubbed his head in thought. "If

there was just some way to distract him. Like with a Frisbee."

"Frisbees go right through him," Malcolm reminded Dandy.

"What we need is a ghost cat," Dandy said. "That would keep him busy."

Malcolm nodded. "Or another dog to distract him."

After a moment, Dandy lit up, giving Malcolm an award-winning grin. "I've got an idea." He pointed to the overhead projector.

Making sure no living person was lurking nearby, Malcolm and Dandy pulled the projector out of the corner and plugged it in. Dandy flipped the switch, causing a large lighted square to appear on the wall.

"Watch this," he said. Dandy moved

his hands in front of the projector, making a doggie shadow puppet. He even added sound effects. "Yip! Yip!" he imitated.

That got Spooky's attention. *Yip! Yip!* he barked back.

"Keep him busy," Malcolm said. "I'll go see if I can find our ghost."

"Wait," Dandy called. "When you leave with the specter detector, Spooky will disappear. I won't be able to see him."

Malcolm looked at Spooky, who seemed to be smitten with Dandy's shadow dog. "As long as you keep that up, he'll be here. I'm going to go find our fisherman."

Making sure no one was in the hall, Malcolm slipped out. He aimed the ghost detector into the teachers' workroom. Nothing. Then he tried the boys' restroom. Still nothing. Then Malcolm

did the bravest thing he'd ever done—he aimed it into the girls' restroom. Nothing there either.

Malcolm slowly made his way to the library. He passed Mrs. Goolsby's room. Strangely, she wasn't there. Malcolm had imagined that she stayed at school late into the night, working on massive piles of lesson plans. Mrs. Goolsby wasn't there. But someone else was.

In the corner by the American flag, stood the fisherman. On the classroom whiteboard he'd written *TELL NO ONE!* over and over, like a kid punished for doing something wrong.

Malcolm carefully approached. "H-h-hello," he muttered.

The fisherman turned toward him. He eyed Malcolm for a moment and then asked, "Can I trust you?"

Malcolm nodded. He wanted to say *yes*, but his throat felt cottony and dry. He didn't think he'd ever get used to being able to talk to ghosts. He just kept nodding his head.

"This is extremely important," the fisherman said.

Malcolm tried to sound brave. "Wh-wh-who are you?"

The fisherman pointed to the words he'd written on the whiteboard. "This is extremely important."

"Okay," Malcolm said.

The ghost took a step closer.

"I need—"

"Excuse me!"

Malcolm jumped. He whipped around at the voice. It was the teacher who'd let him in.

"I said in and out," she nagged. "Let's get a move on."

Malcolm glanced over his shoulder. The fisherman had disappeared. He shut off his detector and walked out. After rescuing Dandy, the boys hopped on their bikes and left empty-handed.

Solving One Problem, Creating Another

Malcolm couldn't concentrate on his homework. His mind kept drifting back to his brief encounter with the fisherman. Malcolm had learned two things.

1. Dandy can do an incredible shadow puppet.

2. The ghost at school had something extremely important to say.

He had to find out what. But once he found out, would he be able to tell anyone? *TELL NO ONE!* He went to bed, still pondering what he should do.

The next morning, Malcolm felt like a zombie. He stumbled through his morning routine, which consisted of eating his cereal while avoiding his sister. He had enough problems without listening to hers. He headed out to the bus in a daze.

Mrs. Goolsby's grating voice woke him with a jolt. "Class," she started, "I've been easy on you until now. But let's face it, summer vacation is over. We've had a couple of days to adjust. It's time to get back to work."

Malcolm glanced at Dandy, whose face had turned the color of plaster.

Mrs. Goolsby continued. "I expect the best from this class. That's why we're going to do some extra math drills this

morning. Please pull out your textbooks and turn to the problems at the end of the chapter. We'll do a few on the board first. Then you'll do the rest on your own. And it will be timed!"

Dandy's face now turned whiter than any ghost they'd encountered.

"Let's start with the first problem. Malcolm, please come up and work it on the board."

Malcolm slipped out of his desk, carrying his math book. He looked at the whiteboard. It was mostly covered with schedules, lesson plans, and quiz dates.

Only one small section was left clean. That was the same section the fisherman had used to write his message. Malcolm slowly picked up a marker. If he snapped a picture of the whiteboard right now, would the messages appear on film? Probably.

He couldn't be concerned with that. He had a major math problem to solve right now. He could solve the ghost problem later.

Malcolm scribbled the problem on the board. *Five hundred and eighty people went to the mall on Saturday. Twice as many people went to the mall on Sunday. How many people went to the mall for the entire weekend?*

As he worked the problem, Malcolm couldn't help but think those 580 people were all clones of his sister, Cocoa, the Mall Queen!

He finished and faced Mrs. Goolsby. She addressed the class. "Do we all agree with Malcolm's answer?"

Most of the students nodded. A few gave a halfhearted, "Yes."

"You may take your seat," Mrs. Goolsby told him.

She didn't have to tell him twice. He grabbed his textbook and hurried back to his seat.

As he scooted by, something fell from the back of his math book and fluttered to the floor. Mrs. Goolsby bent down to retrieve it.

"You dropped this," she said, strolling over to Malcolm's desk. Just before handing it over, she looked at it. It was the picture Malcolm had taken of the fisherman by the marquee.

Mrs. Goolsby's mouth dropped open, her face went pale, and she fainted on the spot.

Identified

After a huge commotion in the classroom, someone ran for help. Another teacher hurried in and helped Mrs. Goolsby up. She saw the picture again, then *bam!* fainted a second time. The nurse came in next and helped Mrs. Goolsby out of the room.

"I need to lie down," Mrs. Goolsby said, holding the back of her hand to her forehead. The nurse tucked the picture into her pocket to hide it from the teacher's view.

Malcolm waited. Minutes passed. The class sat quietly, as instructed, working the rest of the math problems. Malcolm held his pencil, pretending to work. He knew what was coming.

After minutes that felt like hours, a voice came over the speaker. "Malcolm Stewart please report to Mrs. Bergen's office." Mrs. Bergen . . . the principal!

Dandy gave Malcolm a "good luck" look as he walked out.

"Take a seat," Mrs. Bergen, instructed.

Malcolm sat.

Mrs. Bergen was holding the picture. She glanced at it, then at Malcolm, then back at the photo.

Malcolm wished Dandy was there to back him up. How on earth was he going

to explain this?   And even more important, why was Mrs. Bergen not rattled at seeing a ghost!

"I understand you're on the yearbook staff this year," Mrs. Bergen said, her voice steady.

"Yes," Malcolm answered.

He remembered his idea to swap Mrs. Bergen's head with the school mascot. Maybe he should scrap that plan.

"And you brought your camera to school for that reason?" she went on.

"Yes." *Gulp.* Malcolm's throat was so dry it felt like he was swallowing dust.

"While we appreciate your efforts," she droned, "I may have to call your parents about this."

Malcolm tried not to look as confused

as he felt. Call his parents? Because he took a picture of a ghost?

"I'm aware of all the fancy trick photography programs for computers," she said. "But Malcolm, what you did to Mrs. Goolsby was a terrible joke. Do you understand that?"

Malcolm shook his head in confusion. He didn't understand anything!

"Now, I don't know how you found a photo of him. Frankly, I don't want to know. But putting her missing husband into a picture, then making sure she saw it—" She stopped speaking and clenched her fists as though to steady her words. "It's a prank of the cruelest sort."

What? Malcolm's brain tried to compute what he was hearing. *The fisherman was Mrs. Goolsby's husband?*

"B-but—," Malcolm sputtered.

Mrs. Bergen raised her palm up like a crossing guard demanding him to halt. "I don't want to hear it." She took a deep breath. "You owe Mrs. Goolsby an apology. Follow me."

Mrs. Bergen rose and motioned for Malcolm to follow. He trudged along behind her. A couple of quick turns led them into the school clinic.

Mrs. Goolsby was lying down holding the photo, an ice pack on her forehead.

Malcolm approached his teacher, his head down. "Mrs. Goolsby, I'm so sorry that picture upset you."

"I don't want an apology, Malcolm. I want an explanation. My husband left for a fishing trip five years ago . . . just two days before our wedding anniversary. He never returned. How on earth did you get this picture of him?"

"Mrs. Goolsby," Malcolm began.

"And how did you know he called me Noonie?"

"Noonie?" Malcolm's head snapped up. He stared hard at Mrs. Goolsby. He had no idea what she meant.

"Yes. My husband called me Noonie. He nicknamed me that because we first met

each other at the college diner right at noon. So, he always spelled it N-O-O-N-E."

TELL NO ONE! TELL NOONE!

Now Malcolm got it. "I promise, Mrs. Goolsby, I didn't tamper with that photo. That's how it came out."

He had no choice but to tell the truth. He hoped she'd believe him. "I think your husband is trying to tell you something."

Mrs. Goolsby glanced at the picture, then at Malcolm. She sat up, leaning closer to him.

"What do you think he's trying to tell me?" she whispered.

"I don't know. Let's find out," Malcolm whispered back.

Happy Anniversary!

Malcolm went back to the classroom to retrieve his camera. The class was now being led by a substitute teacher.

"Excuse me," he interrupted, "I need Daniel to come with me. . . . " He held up the camera. "For official school business."

The sub nodded.

Dandy sheepishly got up from his desk. His face had turned a carsick green.

"I'm in trouble too?" Dandy asked when they reached the hall.

"No, but I may need you to back me up, in case things don't go as planned."

"What plan?" Dandy slowed his steps.

"Just come on," Malcolm said.

Dandy looked even sicker when he saw Mrs. Goolsby waiting for them.

"Follow me," Malcolm told them.

The three walked out the front door and over to the school's marquee. Malcolm took a quick picture. He checked the camera to make sure what he needed was there. "We'll be able to see it better after we upload it to a computer."

It didn't take long.

"It's the fisherman," Dandy said. "I thought we weren't supposed to tell. Why are we showing Mrs. Goolsby?"

Malcolm smiled. "Well, it turns out we were supposed to tell a certain Noone."

"Huh?" Dandy asked.

"I'll explain later," Malcolm said. "Now look closely. Do you see what I see?"

The photo clearly showed Mrs. Goolsby's husband pointing to the marquee. It now read: *Noone, I'm sorry I missed our anniversary. Check the pocket of my gray jacket. The one I wore when we were married.*

Mrs. Goolsby looked like she may faint a third time. Instead, she excused herself. "You boys go back to class. I think I'll go home for the day."

Malcolm took more pictures around school that afternoon. Mostly banners and bulletin boards, anything with writing on it. But they all came out just as

they were originally written. No special messages. No fisherman.

The next morning, Malcolm and Dandy heard an odd noise coming from their classroom. They cautiously approached the door. The fisherman ghost may have been friendly before, but maybe he had more to say.

When they peeked around the door, they found Mrs. Goolsby humming! She wore a smile as bright as the gleaming diamond necklace around her neck. She brightened even more when she saw Malcolm.

"Malcolm, may I speak to you for a moment?" she asked him.

Malcolm glanced at Dandy. Then he approached Mrs. Goolsby's desk.

"Thank you," she whispered, pointing to the necklace. "I found it in my

husband's jacket pocket, along with a lovely anniversary card."

Malcolm wasn't sure exactly what to say. "It's pretty."

"Yes . . . yes, it is," she agreed. "I'll never know what happened to my husband, but at least now I know he loved me. I have you to thank for that."

Malcolm blushed. Then Mrs. Goolsby let him go back to his desk. He dug in his desk for his math book to get ready for more punishing days of problems.

Malcolm waited for the ruler to snap the class to attention, but that day Mrs. Goolsby waited until after the announcements to begin the lessons.

"I think rather than doing problems," she began, "today we'll begin with a math game."

"A game?" Dandy dared to ask.

"Yes," Mrs. Goolsby answered, all smiles. "Learning doesn't always have to be hard work."

Malcolm pulled out some paper and a pencil. *What a difference a ghost can make,* he thought. Maybe it would be a great school year after all.

FIVE MORE WAYS TO DETECT A GHOST, SPIRIT, OR POLTERGEIST

From Ghost Detectors Malcolm and Dandy

11. Spirits can be found anywhere. So, be on the lookout for ghosts everywhere you go. Keep your ghost detector handy at all times.

12. Ghost hunters often use electronic devices to find ghosts. Use your camera or a recording device to search for spirits.

13. Take Polaroids and digital photos to get quick pictures of spirits.

14. Carefully check your pictures for bright spots called orbs. Some people think these spots show poltergeists.

15. Like Mr. Goolsby, some ghosts are trying to send a message. Just in case, turn on your specter detector and wait for the bleep! When the ghost appears, don't be afraid to say hi!